The Matchmakers

The Matchmakers

Janette Oke

Thorndike Press • Chivers Press
Thorndike, Maine USA   Bath, England

This Large Print edition is published by Thorndike Press, USA and by Chivers Press, England.

Published in 2001 in the U.S. by arrangement with Bethany House Publishers.

Published in 2001 in the U.K. by arrangement with Bethany House Publishers.

U.S. Hardcover   0-7862-3256-0   (Christian Romance Series Edition)
U.K. Hardcover 0-7540-4523-4 (Chivers Large Print)
U.K. Softcover   0-7540-4524-2 (Camden Large Print)

The text of this Large Print edition is unabridged. Other aspects of the book may vary from the original edition.

Set in 18 pt. Plantin by Al Chase.

Printed in the United States on permanent paper.

British Library Cataloguing in Publication Data available

Library of Congress Cataloging-in-Publication Data
Oke, Janette, 1935–
    The matchmakers / Janette Oke.
        p.   cm.
    ISBN 0-7862-3256-0 (lg. print : hc : alk. paper)
    1. Widows — Fiction.   2. Widowers — Fiction.
    3. Fathers and daughters — Fiction.   4. Mothers and sons — Fiction.   5. Domestic fiction, Canadian.
    6. Christian fiction, Canadian.   7. Large type books.
    I. Title.
    PR9199.3.O38 M38 2001
    813'.54—dc21   2001027104

Dedicated with love
to the "special gals"
of the Tuesday morning group,
Ladies Time Out,
of the
Parkdale Evangelical Missionary
Church

God bless!

Contents

Chapter One

The Seed of an Idea

"I don't know what to do."

The words were spoken with such wistfulness that Judith Wright's head came up and she stared across the table at her longtime friend. They were at the Koffee Kup, their usual Saturday morning meeting place, and Judith had just finished fingering up the crumbs of her prune Danish. With one finger aloft, still damp from her last lick, she stared at Cynthia Longley, waiting for some explanation of the problem. When there was no further comment, simply a deep sigh, Judith lowered her finger and leaned forward, concern further deepening her chocolate brown eyes.

"What's wrong?"

Cynthia glanced up from the coffee cup she absentmindedly twisted round and round.

"Oh, nothing's wrong," she was quick to state.

Judith slumped in relief. "You gave me a start."

"I'm sorry. I didn't mean . . ." The words trailed off.

It wasn't like Cynthia to look so melancholy. She was back to fingering the cup again.

"Something is wrong, isn't it?"

"Not . . . not really wrong. It's just that Daddy . . ."

"I thought you and your father were . . . well, close," Judith prompted when Cynthia didn't continue.

"Oh, we are." Cynthia seemed to stir herself from her reverie, shifting slightly on the bright yellow chair. "We are," she repeated more firmly.

Judith stirred, too, not convinced that all was well. She had every intention of finding out exactly what was going on.

"I don't understand," she began, a frown creasing her otherwise smooth forehead. "What's bothering you? C'mon, spill it." She looked intently into the pretty oval face, framed with soft, honey-blond hair.

"I'm not . . . not bothered. I'm just —"

"You're bothered. It's written all over you. Hey, Cynthie. This is me you're talking to. I know when you're bothered."

Cynthia sighed again, then shrugged. They both knew she did not easily hide her thoughts, her emotions, from anyone — particularly Judith. They had known each other too long. Had shared too many secrets. Too much intimacy. Judith in her own probing way could always pry the information from her.

"I feel guilty even sharing this," Cynthia acknowledged, "and I wouldn't . . . to anyone else. I know that everyone thinks, well, that Daddy and I are . . . that I'm so very

— what — ? Blessed? To have Daddy. And they're right," she hurried on before Judith could make any comment. "I know that. I don't know what I would have done, how we ever would have managed, or made it without him since . . . since Roger died, but lately . . ."

She let the words drop and lowered her gaze.

Judith, more than anyone else, knew how difficult the last three years since Roger's sudden death had been for Cynthia. She had hoped that the worst was over. That the painful loss of her husband was behind her in more than just time, that Cynthia was now ready to go on with her life.

Cynthia determinedly pushed the coffee cup away but began to toy with the spoon. It made little clinking sounds on the hard surface of the table, and Judith wanted to reach out and silence its intrusion in the conversation. At last she could stand it no longer and leaned forward, one hand pressing Cynthia's fingers and the annoying clatter of the spoon firmly against the table.

Cynthia's eyes lifted and she stirred restlessly. Her face flushed slightly. "I feel like a real . . . jerk, even thinking like this," she berated herself, "but sometimes . . . sometimes I just feel *smothered.*"

"Smothered?"

"He's always there. Every evening . . . every Saturday. On Sunday. I know the boys have needed him. *I've* needed him. But now . . . I just feel like I'd like a little more breathing space." She stopped and lifted troubled eyes. "I wish he'd let go. Do you know what I'm trying to say?"

Judith was beginning to get the picture. She loved her own father dearly, but she was glad she didn't need to live with him. That her mother was there to be the buffer to his moods. The salve that soothed all agitations. She nodded slowly. She hadn't thought of Cynthia's situation in that light before.

"Can you just sort of ask for a little privacy?" she ventured.

"Oh, Jude, I . . . I couldn't. I wouldn't want Daddy to feel that he's not wanted. Not appreciated. He's been so sweet. I don't know how we ever would have managed. He's been so . . . so gentle with me. I'm sure that's why he agreed to take that early retirement package last spring. He

didn't really want to quit work. He did it so he would have more time for us. He has been so good with the boys. He says over and over how important it is for boys to have a male image to look up to. He's — it's almost like a broken record at times. But he's right. It is. They do. I know that. Sports and fishing. Camping. All those —" She stopped abruptly and shrugged again.

"And he does all those little mannish chores and fix-it jobs," she continued. "You know. He keeps an eye on the furnace filters and gets salt for the . . . something-or-other. And he checks the . . . the oil in the car and tests the tires with that funny little gizmo. I would never have known about all those things, and even if I did know, I'd never have the time to do them. What with working full time and trying to keep up at home and . . . everything."

Judith took another sip of coffee, nodding in understanding above the rim of her cup. She wouldn't know how to manage all of those things either.

"But now I think it's . . . well, it's time for a change," Cynthia continued. "I think maybe I'm ready now. Well . . . not really ready. Some days I wonder if I'll ever be ready. If I'll ever truly adjust to life without —"

" 'Course you will," Judith filled in quickly. "It takes time. Don't rush yourself."

Cynthia sighed deeply. She began to fidget with the coffee spoon again. "Honestly . . ." she said in a soft voice. "Sometimes I feel . . . confined. Hardly able to breathe."

Judith nodded toward the waitress in the bright checked apron and pushed Cynthia's cup to the edge of the table to join her own. They were silent while the waitress replenished both cups, the hot stream sending little shivers of steam upward. Judith added a trace of cream and began to stir. Cynthia tested hers gingerly, taking a small sip, then set the cup on the napkin for a brief cooling time.

"Why don't you just tell him?" Judith asked. The matter seemed really quite simple.

Cynthia looked shocked. "Oh, I couldn't," she exclaimed.

"You think he'd misunderstand?"

"Well, he . . . I'm sure by now he thinks that we . . . He's been looking after us for three years. It would be cruel to just upset everything."

Judith nodded, then leaned slightly toward the coffee before her to make the most of the delicious aroma. "You know, I've a notion to have another Danish," she mused, but Cynthia was quick to cut in.

"You can't. We took the pledge."

"But surely —"

"Only one. One a Saturday. We promised to hold each other to it. Don't try to fudge."

It was Judith's turn to shrug. She lifted her cup and took a sip of the coffee.

"Have you walked?" Cynthia asked.

Judith raised an eyebrow.

"Have you taken your walk?" The words demanded an accounting.

"What are you, the fat police?"

"Come on, Jude. We promised. At

least three times. Have you walked this week?"

"I had to take the dog to the vet. I figured that should count for at least two. Maybe even three. You'll never know how I have to wrestle him to get him into the van."

"Jude!"

"Anyway, that doesn't solve your problem with your father." Judith felt just the slightest twinge of guilt in using her friend's frustration to head her off.

A few moments passed in silence. Cynthia played with the spoon again, and Judith sipped her coffee.

"Couldn't you just . . . talk to him?" Judith picked up the conversation again. "Ask for a little freedom. You know, nothing like, 'There's the door,' or 'We don't want you around anymore.' Just something like . . . like, 'I'm ready to start living again,' or something."

"That's another problem," Cynthia responded slowly. "Some days I think I am ready to . . . to start living. Other days, I'm not sure."

"Then talk to him on your ready day."

"But I can't just say, 'Be there when I need you, and the rest of the time butt out.' "

"Well, it's hardly —"

"It would be. That's just how it would seem to him. What if I . . . if I treated our friendship like that? 'Come when I call. But don't bother on the days I'm feeling I can get by on my own.' "

"Well, you can hardly compare our friendship to —"

" 'Course you can."

"We meet because . . . because we want to meet."

"But we need each other too."

Judith had never really thought of that before. She put her cup down with a dull clunk.

"I mean, I don't know how I'd ever have handled Roger's death without . . . without you there to listen, to cry along with me. I really don't, Jude." Cynthia's eyes glistened with tears.

Judith felt her own eyes threatening to spill over. She nodded. It would be the same for her if something traumatic happened in her life. Cynthia was the one to whom she would turn.

"You'll always have me," Judith said, her voice husky.

"And Daddy too. I don't want him out of my life, Jude. I couldn't . . .

wouldn't want to ever be without him."

Judith nodded. It was a tricky and risky situation.

"Your coffee's getting cold," Judith said, waving toward the untouched cup.

Cynthia moved restlessly. "I shouldn't 've had another cup," she mumbled.

"Well, you've got it. Might as well drink it."

Cynthia obediently took a drink, then set it aside to indicate she had completed her duty. "There's another problem," she said, her eyes clouding. "I'm not quite sure how much Daddy does what he does for us because he knows we need him, or because he needs us."

Judith's eyebrow lifted.

"He's been so lonely since we lost Mama."

"But that's . . . what? Eight years now?"

"Nine. Nine next August."

"Surely he's over it by now."

"Jude, it's not like the measles. You never get over it. Not really. It's always there. The ache. The loneliness. The feeling of being . . . robbed. The pain gets less, but the . . . the hurt never goes away."

With a slight nod Judith acknowledged the fact that she knew nothing about losing a mate. Again her heart ached for her friend.

"So you think your dad is . . . hanging around because he's lonely himself?"

"Well, I know he was terribly lonely after Mama died. I knew that at the time, but I never realized just how lonely until I went through it myself. I feel so bad that I wasn't there for him. I was — or thought I was — so busy with my new marriage, then the little boys. I never really knew what he was going through. And he doesn't talk much about feelings and such things."

"Men never do."

"Well, I suppose not. Roger was a little better than Daddy, though." Cynthia reached again for her coffee cup. She took a sip, then set the cup back down on the shiny table surface. Lukewarm coffee was quite awful, her expression said.

"You should have drunk it earlier like I told you." Judith smiled and shook her head at her friend. Then she said, "So what are you going to do?"

26

Cynthia stood, indicating it was time for her to be off. "I've no idea," she said with another sigh. "I know I won't chance hurting Daddy. Even if he decided to move in with me and the boys. He's been so sweet. I guess we'll just keep on . . ."

"You mean do nothing?" Judith said as she stood, picked up her purse, and reached inside for her billfold. It was her turn to pay. "That doesn't sound like much of a solution."

"Maybe there isn't a solution. Maybe I don't even need a solution. Maybe I should be just plain thankful that I've got a daddy who cares. Who looks after me and the kids. I don't know. Maybe I'm unappreciative. Restless. Selfish."

"You're none of those things and you know it."

27

"Maybe it's a stage one goes through. I don't know. I'm so confused."

"Have you talked with Pastor?"

"Pastor Lawrence must be tired of my face. I spent so much time in his office that first year. It's time to let someone else benefit from his counsel. Surely . . . surely I should be ready to . . . to —"

"Don't rush —" Judith stopped when she remembered she had already said that. But Cynthia didn't seem to notice and picked up on the word.

"Rush?" she repeated. "I don't know the meaning of the word. Seems I have been dragging my feet the whole way but now —"

"Now you are ready . . . for a little space," Judith added encouragingly.

28

"I . . . think so. I need to . . . to discover who I am since . . . since all this happened. See if there is still a person in there somewhere."

"You're going to have to talk with him, Cynthie."

"I can't. I just can't."

"Then just keep on praying. I'll pray, too. Something will turn up. God does have an answer."

"And even that thought scares me," Cynthia said, drawing on a glove. "I don't . . . don't want Him to take Daddy from my life entirely."

Judith's soft chuckle sent her eyes to sparkling. Cynthia looked uncertain, but then joined in. "I know," she admitted sheepishly. "I'm just plain silly. God has been with me even when I didn't know it. I need to trust Him with this too."

Judith nodded and tried again. "There is a solution."

"Like?" The laughter had faded from Cynthia's eyes. She busied herself with pressing each finger firmly into the glove of her right hand with the fingers of her left.

"I don't know. Maybe marriage?"

"Marriage? I'm not ready for marriage."

Judith looked at Cynthia evenly as she shrugged into her denim jacket. "Maybe not," she said with a teasing twinkle. "But what about your dad?"

"Oh, Jude! That's preposterous!"

"Hurry. We'll be late," eight-year-old Todd called out to his brother, his voice filled with concern.

Cynthia sighed. It was Friday, and the morning had been typical —

Todd fussing and six-year-old Justin dawdling. She wished, as often, that she had a better match in her pair. Todd was such a perfectionist, so impatient. Justin was easily distracted and plodding. It was not a good mix for tranquility.

"We'll be late for sure," Todd was pronouncing in his prediction-of-doom voice.

Justin slowly reached for his other boot. Halfway there his hand changed its mind and somehow ended up holding a small Matchbox car instead.

"Justin," Cynthia was forced to intervene. "We do need to hurry. Leave the car until after school."

Obediently the young boy set aside the car and took up the other boot.

With a shake of her head Cynthia

31

turned back to gathering her gloves, purse, and car keys. She wished they didn't have to go through this little ordeal every school morning.

Her next thought brought a smile to her lips. Just like their parents, the two of them. When she and Roger had first married, their two different personalities often meant discord. She had been the impatient one, always standing, shifting from one foot to the other, trying vainly to hurry him. He had only smiled, teased her a bit, and continued to take his own sweet time. They had needed to work it out. They talked it over, and she tried to slow down. Roger worked ahead to gather those things he would need when leaving the house so there wouldn't be any last-minute delays. It mostly had worked. Harmony was restored.

After the babies arrived, she was the one who held up their departures, but Roger came through again and assumed the role of gatherer. While she bundled little ones, he stuffed diaper bags with all the miscellaneous items that babies and new mamas seem to need.

Cynthia stirred from her reverie and turned back to her sons. Justin was finally zipping up his jacket. Todd was standing with the door held open, even though the morning held a sharp chill. "We'll be late," he said again in a dull voice, impatience causing a deep frown to crease his forehead.

"Never been late yet," responded Justin.

Todd scowled. "You would be late lots of times if I didn't make you hurry."

Justin shrugged his shoulders and grinned.

Finally they were out the door and in the car. Cynthia felt that the worst part of her morning was over. Dealing with customers at the bank where she worked was easy in comparison.

"Is Grandpa Paul comin' for dinner?" asked Justin.

" 'Course. He always does," responded Todd before Cynthia could even open her mouth.

"I hope he got my watch fixed."

"What's wrong with your watch?" Cynthia had heard nothing about a broken watch.

"He broke it going down the slide backward," put in Todd.

"It caught when I fell," Justin said simply.

The watch had been her father's

idea. With a timepiece to make the boy more aware of fleeting moments, Justin might realize that there were times when hurrying was perfectly in order. It hadn't worked. But Justin loved the watch. It was his prized possession.

"What broke?"

"Just the strap piece. Just a little bit. Grandpa Paul will fix it."

Yes, thought Cynthia. Grandpa Paul will fix it. Grandpa Paul fixes everything . . . well, just about everything.

Cynthia's eyes teared up. What on earth was she thinking? What ever would she do without her father?

"I'm gonna ask him if we can go ice-fishing tomorrow. Darren's dad is takin' him ice-fishin'," continued Justin.

"It's too cold for ice-fishing," Cynthia said as she negotiated a corner, her eyes on the road.

"No, it's not. You wear your warm clothes — an' jump an' run around on the ice to keep warm an' stuff."

"I thought maybe you'd like to go with me to the craft show."

"Craft shows are for girls." This from Todd who had gender roles well sorted.

"There's a whole section there for kids," Cynthia corrected.

"Girl kids."

"Not girl kids. There are —"

"I'd rather go with Grandpa Paul," Justin said simply.

"You don't even know if he's going anyplace," Todd reminded him. "He hasn't said that he's going ice-fishing."

"I'll just stay home with him, then." The matter was settled as far as Justin was concerned.

"Maybe we can go to the craft show for a few minutes after church on Sunday," Cynthia suggested hopefully. She wanted some time with her sons but could think of nothing they could do together in the dead of winter.

"Grandpa said he'd help me build my new model," Todd announced. "He said we'd start right after dinner."

So the plans for Sunday had already been made as well.

Cynthia eased the car up against the curb. "Get out on the sidewalk," she cautioned as she always did when she let them out at school.

"Bye, Mom."

Todd was gone almost before she had completely stopped the car. Justin leaned forward to plant a moist kiss on her cheek. "Bye, Mom." Then he slowly began to gather his lunch box, reader, mitts, and scarf. "Bye, Mom," he called again before he shut the door, then stood, belongings dangling, mitts held in his hands instead of on them. "Bye, Mom," he called again, struggling to wave with hands full of little-boy school items.

He's going to lose another mitt, thought Cynthia, shaking her head and smiling at him. *He's already been through three pairs this winter.*

He stood and waited. She knew he would not leave to trudge toward the school building until he had watched her pull away. With a last wave and a thrown kiss, she eased the car back out into the street. *Such a little guy. Such a sweet little guy. And so much like his daddy.*

She felt cheated that she wouldn't get to spend more time with him on the weekend. She had so little time with him anymore, and he wouldn't be her little boy for long.

"You going to the craft show today?" Judith asked as they sat at the Koffee Kup the next morning.

Cynthia shook her head. "I don't think so. I had thought the boys might like to go. See some of the models and things."

"They don't?"

"Daddy took them ice-fishing."

"Ice-fishing? Isn't it a bit cold for that?"

"That's what I thought. But they

took a thermos of hot chocolate and lots of sandwiches. If they get cold, they'll go to the diner just off the lake. They have video games there. Todd is crazy about video games."

"Why don't you go anyway?"

"To the craft show?" Cynthia shook her head. "Not much fun going alone. I've decided to stay home and catch up on some of my cleaning."

"Not much fun cleaning alone either," said Judith dryly.

Cynthia smiled and nodded her agreement. She turned back to the topic of the craft show. "You going?"

"Yeah. Soon as I get home from grocery shopping. Why don't you come with us?"

Cynthia was uncertain. "Taking the kids?"

"We're all going. Cal says I just take

him along to tote the things I buy, but he does a bit of buying himself. Last year he bought this humongous birdhouse. We could hardly get it in the van. The kids had to sit all cramped in there around the big thing. Not a single bird used it all summer, but it does look cute. Cal keeps reminding me of that."

Cynthia felt a little twinge somewhere deep inside. It sounded like so much fun to be a family.

"By the way, I asked Cal to sort of . . . keep an eye out. You know, for a nice widow or —"

"Oh, Jude," Cynthia gasped. "You didn't tell him —"

" 'Course not. I told him nothing, except that I thought it would be a wonderful idea if your dad found a nice woman —"

"Oh, Jude. I wish you —"

But Judith was looking at her with an impish grin. "Listen," she said. "If your daddy's lonely, we need to help fix it."

A twinkle shone from her eyes. Some of the distress left Cynthia's mind. Judith always made a game out of life. Crazy Judith. But she had a loving heart. One that sought to take care of friends.

"Well —" Cynthia began, smiling in spite of herself. "Perhaps he isn't that lonely. Maybe he's quite happy the way things are."

Judith reached across the table and took hold of Cynthia's wrist. She gave it a little shake. "You're not going to have a life until he has a life," she said with unusual seriousness.

"I have a life."

"But not the kind of life that you deserve. Not the kind you are . . . wanting. I've been thinking about it ever since our talk. I should have seen it sooner. But I didn't. Cynthie, you are left out of everything. The Couples Club because you aren't a couple, the Mom's Day Out because you are working, the Valentine Dinner because you don't have a Valentine, and it goes on and on."

"But how will marrying off my daddy change any of that?" asked Cynthia bluntly.

Judith shook her head. "I'm not sure," she admitted, "but we have to take things one step at a time."

"Sure. Take away my built-in baby-sitter and I'll never get out of the house — not even for shopping."

"You can leave the kids with Cal.

He'd never notice he had another two there. I think he just lets them go, anyway, the way the house looks sometimes when I get back home. Good thing it's a mess to begin with. At least I don't notice much difference."

Cynthia smiled again and picked a cherry from her Danish. Judith was not a fussy housekeeper, but her home never looked that bad.

"Anyway, I told Cal to just . . . sort of keep his eyes and ears open. And don't 'Oh, Jude' me."

"He . . . he won't say anything to anybody, will he?"

"Cal? Never. He's about as close-lipped as the proverbial clam. Even I have to pry things from him."

"But —"

"But he's observant. And he understands people. It amazes me, the little things that he picks up. Should have been a detective or something. Details fly right over my head, but Cal seems to see and hear everything that's going on. Little things. Not just what people do, but why. I never catch those things. I just take things as they come — on the surface. Never notice the deeper side." Judith used her hands expressively to emphasize her comments.

Cynthia nodded and smiled. It was true. Judith was an everything-on-the-surface person. One knew exactly what she was thinking or feeling about any subject. She took others in the same way — on the surface. While she, Cynthia, was more inclined to bury things. To feel things deeply yet silently. Judith was never silent.

Cynthia often wondered if she talked to herself if no one else was around.

Judith waved for a refill of her coffee cup. "Cal will watch. But no one — not a soul — will realize that he is watching. He's like that."

"I'm not sure Daddy —"

"Cal will never let your daddy know, and he certainly will not try to make a match. Never. You know Cal better than that. He'd never interfere."

"Then what — ?"

"Sometimes folks can sit right beside each other and never catch on that they would be good for each other. Sometimes folks just need a little nudge."

"And who's going to do the nudging?" Cynthia asked with some trepidation.

Judith smiled. "Well . . . I'm not above a little nudging."

With fresh cups of coffee they settled back for a few moments of quiet reflection. Cynthia was the first to speak.

"I sure don't want Daddy pushed into something."

"Nobody will do any pushing, Cynthie. Promise. There's a big difference between pushing and encouraging."

"I don't know . . ."

"Relax. Maybe Cal won't even be able to come up with a good prospect. We won't force the issue, you know."

Uneasiness still made Cynthia shift slightly. *Force the issue,* her thoughts repeated. *No. No one will force Daddy. He has a mind of his own. Always has.* She supposed that he was safe enough. She managed a weak smile and turned back to her Danish. She would try to put the whole conversation out of her mind.

"If you happen to see any of those knitted dishcloths at the craft sale, would you pick me up a couple? Mine are getting pretty ratty looking."

"Daddy, that button looks about to come off," Cynthia said, indicating a dangling button on her father's sweater.

He followed her gaze. "So it is," he responded. With one quick little jerk he finished the job, tucking the button into his pocket.

"Want me to sew it on?"

"I can do it when I get home."

"I'll do it now, if you like."

He reached back into his pocket

and produced the button. "Would you? I hate sewing buttons. Would rather change a tire, or pull a pump, than sew on a button."

Cynthia waited while he removed his sweater and handed it to her with the button. "That was always your mother's job," he explained unnecessarily.

"I know."

She saw the wistfulness in his eyes. She knew he was still lonely. He had adjusted in many ways. But one could never really adjust to the loneliness. Maybe, just maybe, Judith was right. It was possible her father did need someone. Someone to share his days and his long evenings. Someone to help with the little chores of daily living. Someone to care whether he came home.

As Cynthia sewed on the button, her thoughts traveled to areas she had not allowed them to go to for many months. *Maybe I've been selfish,* she concluded. *Maybe Daddy is longing for a life of his own but feels that he has to stay and care for me and the boys. Maybe I need to let* him *go.*

The unexpected twist in her thinking brought tears to her eyes.

Chapter Two

A Plan of Action

"I think I'll have the sesame bagel."

Judith's head came up from the coffee she was stirring. "What do you mean — sesame bagel? You never have the sesame bagel. What happened to the fruit Danish?"

Cynthia shrugged. "I just feel like having something different."

Judith shrugged too. "Well, make mine the raspberry Danish," she informed the young woman who waited for their orders. "I'm sure what was good last week will be good this week too."

Cynthia felt that the glance thrown her way held a bit of reproof. "I didn't say I was trading in my kids," she stated with some annoyance, "just ordering a sesame bagel."

"You're getting restless," Judith countered.

"Not restless. I've been having a fruit Danish for years."

"That's just the point. Why — ?"

"Do I have to go on ordering the same thing every Saturday for the rest of my life?" she asked, agitation giving an edge to her voice. She stared at Judith, her jaw set. Why are we even

54

discussing this? she wanted to say.

Judith stared back, then laughed.

It began as a funny little snort and quickly turned into full hilarity. Soon the two of them were sharing the mirth of the silly exchange. They hadn't laughed like that since they had been college roomies.

"Have all the sesame bagels you want — and English muffins, too, if it pleases you," Judith gasped out. "I'm glad to see you are able to make changes."

"I'm in a rut. My whole life is in a rut," said Cynthia, wiping at the laughter tears in her eyes.

"Maybe life is nothing but ruts. Comfortable ruts — when things go well. Jarring ruts — when things go wrong. I don't know. We sort of settle in and feel content with the familiar

— even when the familiar is not what we really want from life. Are we really that fearful of change, Cynthie? Boy! I hadn't realized — my rut is getting pretty deep. I really should do something to shake things up. Wish I would have ordered the . . . the cherry cheesecake or —"

"Not the cheesecake. Too many calories."

Judith frowned. "I forgot for a moment. I'm out with the fat patrol."

They laughed again, not as boisterously as before.

"You said you had some news," Cynthia prompted as the waitress placed steaming cups before them.

"Wish I'd have just had Columbian," stated Judith, frowning at her coffee mocha. "Been having the same —"

"Jude! You said you had news about something."

Judith's eyes lifted to look into Cynthia's face. Her whole countenance brightened. "Oh, I have," she enthused. "I could hardly wait to tell you. You know — what's his name? That lawyer, the one who sits at church over there on the left — by the Lairds?"

"Attorney," corrected Cynthia. "He wishes to be called an attorney — not lawyer."

"What's the difference? He's in law, isn't he?"

Cynthia shrugged. "I dunno. Folks say he doesn't like to be called a lawyer. That's all I know."

"What's his name?"

Cynthia thought for a few moments. She couldn't remember.

"I think it's — what's that big law firm in the city?" Judith tried again. "He's connected with it. You know that big one. You hear the name all the time. Starts with . . . with some direction."

"Direction? You mean East, South — ?"

"West — that's it. He's with Weston," Judith said, triumphant.

"Right. Weston, Weston & Hughes. Is he the Weston or Hughes part?"

"He's Weston. The second Weston. His father was the first Weston. He's gone now. Died about two years ago."

Cynthia's eyes clouded. She still could not hear the words relating to death without pain.

"So — what about him?" she finally managed.

"Cal has gotten to know him. Racquetball. They play in the same church league. Lately they have been teaming up for doubles. Having coffee after."

Poor Cal, Cynthia wished to say but bit her tongue. That would be unfair. She really didn't know the attorney. But she had to admit that she had never been too impressed with the little she had observed of him.

"Well, listen to this," said Judith, leaning forward, her cheeks flushing with the excitement of her soon-to-be-disclosed news. "He has a mother."

Cynthia frowned.

"He has a mother," repeated Judith.

"I was under the impression that all mortals have mothers," said Cynthia dryly. "I thought it was part of the plan."

"No, silly! He has a mother — widowed."

"So — ?" Cynthia turned palms up to underscore her question.

"He's worried about her. Well . . . concerned anyway. She is planning to come and spend some time with him. She's lonely. They had moved — his mom and dad, just before his father died — to a new area, a new church. She didn't even have time to make another set of friends. He — *Attorney* Weston" — Judith spoke the words with exaggerated emphasis, swaying her shoulders to keep time with each syllable — "is afraid that once she gets here, she'll just stay."

"What's wrong with that? He's single, isn't he? I should think he'd like someone to cook his meals and wash his socks."

"Guess he doesn't."

"So he doesn't want her? His own mother?" It sounded very uncaring to Cynthia.

"He doesn't think that would be good for either of them. He's been on his own since law school."

"I've wondered about that. How come he's not married?"

"I don't know. I've never stopped to think about it." Judith stared at Cynthia, who could feel herself flushing. It wasn't that she had been staying up nights thinking about it either. She just wondered, that's all.

"Why doesn't his mother move back to her old area? Surely her old friends are still there," Cynthia commented.

"He asked her that. She said she

couldn't. Not alone. It just wouldn't be the same."

Cynthia felt her heart going out to the lonely widow. She understood some of those feelings. It wouldn't be the same. But then — nothing was.

"So what — ?" began Cynthia, determinedly bringing her thoughts back to the present conversation.

"You aren't getting it, are you?"

Cynthia shrugged. Judith had lost her — way back on the verbal trail when she had taken one of her unexpected turns.

"No. I guess I'm not. I've no idea —"

"Your father!"

"My — what?"

"Your father. Don't you see? It would be perfect. A widow — a widower. She is —"

"Jude. How could you? I mean —

really. Daddy is not desperate."

"But you are."

The frank statement raised the heat again in Cynthia's cheeks. Her back straightened. "I am *not* desperate," she said firmly.

"Okay, okay. You're not desperate. I'm sorry," Judith quickly amended. "But we had agreed that finding a nice —"

"It was your idea. I hadn't agreed to anything."

"But you didn't oppose it either. Did you?"

"Well I . . . I'm not about to make these kinds of decisions for my father. If he feels that . . ."

Judith looked impatient. "Look. No one is making decisions — just introductions, that's all."

"But —"

"Listen — this lawyer — attorney," Judith quickly corrected herself. "Cal says he's a nice guy."

"He's a stuffed shirt. He looks so solemn all the time you'd think he was in court."

"He's . . . serious."

"Serious? I don't think I've ever seen the man crack a smile. Even when he says good morning, only his lips move. If his mother is anything like that, I'm not sure that I want Daddy —"

"Oh, Cynthie. You're being obstinate."

Their friendship allowed a frankness that was open yet without real condemnation.

"Look — if it was your father, would you want an alliance with the mother of Sober Weston?" asked

Cynthia pointedly.

"Well, I hope that I'd have the good sense to at least meet her first before passing judgment."

The words cooled the fire in Cynthia's heart. She lowered her gaze and began fingering her coffee spoon. At last she looked up, nodded, and admitted sheepishly, "You're right. I have no right to dismiss her when I haven't even met her. And for all that, I don't know him either. Not really."

"Cal says he's got a great sense of humor."

Cynthia wanted to ask where the man kept it hidden, but she did not.

"And he's a great racquetball player. Plays squash too."

"Does his mother?"

Cynthia asked the question teasingly and Judith gave her a playful swat.

"Don't be a simp," she responded. "I think her sport is mountain climbing."

A sudden thought made Cynthia hold her breath. "Cal didn't talk to him about Daddy, did he?"

" 'Course not. He did tell him that our church had a seniors' program that he hoped his mother would try. Get her out a bit. That sort of thing."

Cynthia breathed in relief. She would have been so embarrassed had Cal made her father look like a lonely-heart case.

"On the other hand," Judith went on, her eyes shining again, "who better than your father to introduce her to the group?"

Cynthia was already shaking her

head before the statement was completed. "Oh no."

"What's the matter? Don't you think your father is capable of judging for himself?"

"Of course he is."

"Then what are you afraid of? He's friendly. He knows all the ropes — all the group. He'd be a perfectly logical one to make a new member feel at home."

"Not if . . . not if he's supposed to be a . . . a suitor."

"A suitor? Who said anything about a suitor? All we are going to do is give them a chance to meet each other. That's all." Judith was shaking her head in exasperation.

"And how — ?"

"Well, Cal likes this guy," Judith started out slowly, then warmed to the subject. "Keeps talking about having him in for Sunday dinner. I figured the best time to do that is right after his mother gets here. Sort of . . . make her feel welcomed." She winked.

"And then . . . ?"

"Then it would be perfectly natural for me to also invite my best friend — and her family."

Cynthia only looked at her friend.

"It's the only thing a hospitable churchgoer would do. Isn't it?" went on Judith in a teasing tone.

Cynthia stirred restlessly. It seemed that Judith had the whole thing worked out.

"I don't know, Jude . . ."

"Just keep a Sunday open. She's supposed to be here in a couple of weeks."

For a reason that she could not

have explained, Cynthia still felt un-
settled about the whole thing.

"What are we going to do today?"

Cynthia was not sure if her father
was directing the question to her or to
her sons. She had hoped to spend the
snowy day quietly — perhaps with a
fire in the fireplace, a good book, or
an afternoon of family games. It
seemed a long time since they had
just had fun together. "I know,"
Todd interjected with enthusiasm.
"Let's rent some videos."

"Yeah!" seconded Justin.

"Great!" said her father with a
glance out the window. "It's a perfect
day for videos. Maybe your mother
has some popcorn she could pop."
He cast a glance toward Cynthia as he
made the remark.

"I think I'm all out," Cynthia said, feeling a bit of a letdown as her own plans quickly vanished.

"We'll pick some up while we're out getting the videos," her father offered.

Already the three men of the house were getting into their coats. The usually dawdling Justin seemed in more of a hurry than the other two.

"Do you have lots of milk for hot chocolate?" her father asked as he slipped on his gloves and reached for the car keys he had tossed on the kitchen counter.

"That depends on how much hot chocolate you will be drinking," replied Cynthia evenly. Rather than a relaxed, snuggly day, she now glumly pictured three males stretched out across the family room while she

scurried around in her kitchen keeping them supplied with popcorn and hot chocolate.

"We'd better get some apples, too," put in Justin. "I like apples with my popcorn."

"Anything else?" her father asked.

"I'm going out for groceries anyway. I'll get it," Cynthia told them.

Her father nodded, quite satisfied that everything was arranged.

Cynthia watched them go. The boys were noisy in their excitement, and her father was filled with good-natured gusto. Cynthia knew that her quiet Saturday afternoon was not to be. She mourned just a little bit as she added popcorn, more milk, and apples to her grocery list.

"When did you say this Mrs. Weston is arriving?" Cynthia's query brought Judith's head up.

"Not sure. Soon, I think."

"Hasn't Cal been playing — what — tennisball?"

"Racquetball. Yeah. He plays every Tuesday."

"Hasn't . . . Attorney Weston said anything?"

"I don't know. Cal is — you know — quite uncommunicative. He doesn't say much about things unless I point-blank ask him."

"Well, ask him."

Judith stopped chewing her last bite of toasted scone, her announced venture into variety. "What's going on?" she asked around food in her mouth.

Cynthia flushed. "I just thought that you were — you know — talking about an . . . an introduction, that's all."

"With your father?"

Cynthia nodded. She could not bring herself to give a verbal agreement.

Judith swallowed and leaned forward.

"I had the impression," she began, "that you weren't too crazy about the idea. Cal said, 'Jude, don't push it.

Let things happen as they happen.' So I sort of —"

"But . . . I thought . . ." For a minute Cynthia felt a strange little panic. She needed help. She needed Judith's help. Her friend was right. She would never have a life of her own, a life with her boys, until her father had one.

Cynthia checked herself. That was foolish. Downright foolish. Her father was taking care of them, and she wasn't fully appreciating it. She lowered her head, her cheeks hot with shame.

"I . . . I wasn't thinking that we should 'push it,' " she ventured when she could look up. "But it might not hurt to at least — you know — let them get acquainted. Sort of see what happens. Daddy is a smart and capable man. If she isn't . . . well, right, then he's not about to be tricked into anything."

"You want him to marry?"

"Well, no, not . . . maybe not marry, at least not . . . well, perhaps *see* someone. You know, show a little interest or . . ." Cynthia came to a stammering halt. What exactly did she want?

"I don't know," she finally admitted. "I just . . . just need space. Space to find my family again. To see if I can function as a person. I don't . . . I can't even make decisions anymore. The boys get to decide on more things than I do."

"I hadn't realized —" began Judith.

"Maybe I'm just being silly," Cynthia hurried on. "But I . . . I got rather used to being an adult. I mean, when Roger was here, we made decisions for the family. We had our understanding on the various areas of . . . of being in charge. We told the boys what the day's activities would be. Now I'm not even asked. Daddy thinks — he means to be helping me. But he's . . . he's taking over my home. He's smothering me. I feel I'm not an adult anymore — not a mother. I love my father. I wouldn't know what to do without him, but —"

"You need help," assured Judith with finality.

Cynthia toyed with her cup, her eyes clouded. "Maybe not . . . not marriage," she said when she looked up, "but if you could — even if it would mean a few Saturday outings, I'd —"

"I'll have Cal do some fishing," replied Judith.

"And this . . . this attorney guy — ?"

"Weston. He goes by P.C."

"P.C.? That's rather a strange —"

"That's what I thought. Cal says he doesn't like his name. Was teased horribly when he was a kid."

"What is it? How can it be worse than P.C.? That's —"

"Preston."

"Preston? That's not so bad. Sounds better than P.C."

"Preston Weston?"

"Oh!"

They looked at each other, the glint in their eyes quickly sparking a burst of laughter.

"That's a hoot," said Cynthia when she could finally speak. "Preston Weston. Who ever would name their kid that?"

"Mrs. Weston," replied Judith

around more explosions of mirth.

"Hey, maybe I don't want my father meeting this woman after all," Cynthia added in good humor.

The laughter. It was good for the soul. Cynthia supposed that was the main reason they had stayed friends ever since college. They had always found reason to laugh together. Somehow things just seemed funnier when she had Judith to share them.

"Can't you just hear the kids singsonging that? *Preston Weston. Preston Weston,*" mimicked Judith, rocking school-kid fashion in time to her chant.

Cynthia stopped mid-chuckle. Perhaps it was no laughing matter. "Must have been horrid for him," she said slowly. A strange feeling of compassion washed through her as she thought of a little boy, tormented because of his name. No wonder the man didn't smile much.

"Cynthie."

Her coat sleeve was tugged and she heard her name hissing almost directly in her ear. She turned to find Judith right behind her, leaning slightly over her shoulder, a dancing light causing her dark eyes to flash. "She's here."

Cynthia's eyebrows came together. "Who?"

"The widow."

The widow. Mrs. Weston. The attorney's mother. A feeling of nervousness flooded through Cynthia — a feeling akin to going out on one's first date.

"Where?"

It was only a whisper, but Judith, who had now moved to stand before Cynthia, heard it.

"With him — over on the left side where he always sits." They both looked into the church sanctuary from the foyer.

"What's she . . . like?" Cynthia forced from a dry mouth.

Judith shrugged. "She looks all right."

All right? Cynthia almost said it aloud. *All right is not good enough for Daddy.* But she said nothing. Just worked on swallowing.

"Cal is going to ask them for dinner next Sunday. Are you free?"

"Next Sunday? Shouldn't we sort of get to know her a little bit?"

"I don't know how else to get to know her. Her son has been here for

— what — almost three years? We've never gotten to know him."

Cynthia nodded. It was true. But everything seemed so sudden. She felt nervousness crawl along her spine.

"Are you free?" Judith prompted.

It was a rather silly question. Cynthia was always free on a Sunday. She nodded dumbly.

"Your father?"

"My father — what?"

"Free? Will he be able to come?"

Cynthia swallowed again and nodded her head. Of course her father was free. He never did anything but take dinner with them on a Sunday.

"Good!"

Judith's enthusiasm was far different from what Cynthia was feeling. Her exuberant friend gave her arm a little squeeze, eyes dancing. "We'll do it!" And Judith was gone.

Cynthia wished there were someplace she could be alone. Could just sort of catch her breath, clear her head. But the foyer of the church, filled with the usual rush and vigor of worshipers greeting one another, offered no place of solitude, no time of silence. She stirred, absentmindedly returned "Good mornings" with a forced smile and made her way toward the sanctuary. The boys had already rushed off to their respective classes, but her father would be waiting for her to join him in their usual seat on the right side for the adult Bible class.

A stain of red began to flush her cheeks. Would her father know? Would he, through some mysterious sense, be aware that she was plotting something? How would he feel?

Cynthia steeled herself against her uneasiness and moved forward. She could not leave — would not ever consider it. Perhaps it was the habit of many years that always found her in church each Sunday morning. Perhaps a sense of duty toward her father would not allow her to leave him sitting there alone. Perhaps the unconscious realization that she needed God this morning, needed direction and guidance, drew her toward her usual place.

She eased in beside her father and took a deep breath. As much as she felt compelled to do so, she did not turn and look across the sanctuary to where the Westons sat. Maybe she could not have turned even if she had tried. She wasn't sure. It was enough to sit beside her father, wondering if he sensed a difference in her. She felt anxious every time he stirred.

The Sunday school lesson that morning was on the topic of finding God's will.

Cynthia cringed many times as the teacher, fluently quoting verse after verse, took them on a spiritual quest. Once, only once, did she dare cast a glance toward Judith. Her friend seemed entirely at ease, nodding in agreement at the points being made.

Cynthia lowered her gaze to the Bible in her lap, but the words on the page seemed to blur.

"There are those times when God expects us to move forward," the teacher was saying. "We cannot always sit back and expect Him to do everything on our behalf. Sometimes God needs to almost push us from the nest. Make us test our wings. Grow up and take charge of our life."

Is this one of those times? Cynthia asked herself. *Is God pushing me forward? Making me grow?*

"But we must be careful to be prayerful and obedient to His leading."

Ah — there was the catch. Had she been prayerful? Obedient? Or was she simply taking matters into her own hands?

Cynthia bowed her head and closed her eyes tightly. A heartfelt little prayer rose heavenward. With humility she asked her Father to help her to use wisdom — to stay in step, to accept His will. Tears slipped from the corner of her eyes. She would meddle no more. Unless, of course, she really felt God directing her — no, that was silly. God didn't need her meddling. He was quite able to work things out in His own way.

But Judith? Judith already had things in motion. There was no way for Cynthia to back out now. Was there? No, it wouldn't be fair to Judith.

She would go to dinner next Sunday as promised. But she would do nothing — *nothing* to push her father into any kind of a relationship with the widow woman.

"So what did you think of her?"

Judith's question did not come until the following Saturday when they met for coffee. This time Cynthia understood exactly who she meant. The woman had been on her mind all week. Still, she did not have an answer. "What do you mean? I won't even meet her until tomorrow."

"But what's your impression?"

"You mean — ?"

"How did you think she looked? Oh, I know we're not to judge by . . . by appearance, but you can tell something."

"I didn't see her."

"Didn't see her? She was right there with . . . with P.C."

"I didn't look."

"You didn't! You mean you didn't even look to see what — ?"

"No, I didn't."

"But how could you resist? I mean —"

"Look, Jude, I've . . . I've decided not to get involved. I mean if —"

"You promised. The kids are all

pumped up about having your boys there for dinner. I've made the frozen dessert. Cal has —"

"I'll still come for dinner."

Judith's face showed her relief, but then she frowned. "Just what are you saying?"

"I will come for dinner. I will bring Daddy with me. You may introduce him to . . . to the Westons. But I will not try to manipulate things so . . . so they will — you know."

"I didn't think the intention was ever to do any manipulating. You said yourself that your father would never be pushed into anything."

"I know. But —"

"Then I don't see how you can call inviting people for dinner manipulation or anything like it." Judith's voice held some indignation.

"Well, it's not really — maybe. It's not what we've — what I've done. It's what I *wanted* to do — that's the manipulation."

"And what did you want to do?"

Cynthia blushed. "Cut it out. You know as well as I do."

"Marry off your father so you could have a life," Judith stated simply.

It sounded absolutely awful.

"There's nothing wrong with wanting to be in charge of your own life," Judith continued.

"Yes. Yes, there is. That's just the whole point. God is in charge of my life. I'm not to be taking things into my own hands and trying to work them out to suit my whims."

"This is hardly a whim, Cynthie."

"Well, it is. Really. It's easy to think that I know what's best for me. But only God really knows that. I need to . . . to just trust Him to work things out."

Judith nodded in agreement. "But the dinner is still on?"

Cynthia nodded back. "The dinner — yes. But no funny stuff. No trying to get the two of them off by themselves or —"

"We're not dealing with teenagers here," retorted Judith impatiently. "Nobody's going to try to shove these two mature adults at each other."

"Of course not. I'm sorry. It's just this . . . this whole thing has me sort of on edge. I don't want to jump in and interfere where I have no business. We need God's will in this."

"Listened closely last Sunday, did we?" said Judith, breaking off a section of her orange muffin.

Cynthia could not help but smile. She shrugged. "Okay. So I listened. I think the lesson might have been meant just for me."

"Oh, I needed it a bit too. Cal reminded me of that on the way home."

They looked at each other and shared a grin.

"We'll do the dinner thing —" began Judith.

"And we won't manipulate," added Cynthia.

"And we'll just see what happens with it."

Cynthia nodded. "Deal!"

They turned to their morning pastries and ordered cups of fresh coffee. But it wasn't long until Cynthia noticed an impish smile playing about her friend's mouth.

"What's with you?"

Judith tossed her head. "Nothing."

"There is too. I can see it brewing."

"I was just thinking, wouldn't it be fun if it happened anyway? Without us. Well . . . maybe not totally without us. Maybe we'll need to — you know — give just a wee nudge in the right direction."

"Jude!"

"What? You know perfectly well that sometimes God expects us to do our part."

Judith's eyes were twinkling again. Cynthia knew she was teasing. At least she hoped so.

Chapter Three

Introductions All Around

Cynthia was so uptight that her hands felt clammy. The little glances she kept casting toward her father all the way to the Wrights' house didn't help, even though he seemed perfectly calm. He looked serene, relaxed. *How can he feel so totally at ease with what lies ahead?* she wondered rather illogically. Because, of course, he didn't know. It was only Judith who shared her secret. Maybe Cal. Cal had advised caution. He must know a little about what was being schemed.

In the backseat Todd and Justin were fairly bouncing with excitement. Then Cynthia realized how long it had been since the boys had enjoyed such an outing. That was one more thing she missed because Roger was gone. They were no longer invited out to visit with other families. Not like they used to be when exchanging Sunday dinner invitations was a common occurrence.

Cynthia was wise enough to realize that her father's marriage, should he ever decide to take the plunge sometime in the future, would not change that circumstance. She and her boys still would not be seen as a whole family. Acknowledging the reality made her feel almost panicky. Would she give up her father, only to be even worse off than before? Maybe she should try once more to get out of today's dinner date.

But her father was already easing his Chevy into the Wrights' driveway. A sleek black Olds already occupied the left. The other guests obviously were already being entertained.

Cynthia felt her stomach knot. But already the boys were clambering out of the car. The Wright boys were jumping up and down on the front steps, calling words of boisterous welcome to their friends. There was no turning back now. Cynthia steeled herself and opened her car door.

Cal Wright was standing behind his

excited offspring. He opened the door with a broad smile to welcome his new guests. Cynthia entered the home to which she had been admitted so many times over the years, feeling uncomfortably like a stranger.

Judith had outdone herself, Cynthia noticed. Never had she seen the homey place so polished. No magazines carelessly tossed on the coffee table. No kids' toys under the skirt of the sofa or peeking out from between the cushions. Every piece of furniture was gleaming. Cynthia could still smell the lemon of the furniture polish. And the carpet showed only a few indentations where visitors' feet had made their way to easy chairs.

She must have worked all Saturday, Cynthia told herself and then remembered that Judith had Cal to help her. He was good with the vacuum, Judith had often boasted. Their eldest, Erin, was old enough now to be a real help to her mother with household chores also.

Still, Cynthia knew enough about family life to know that it took effort and organization to get the room so spotless, and even more effort to keep it that way from Saturday to Sunday afternoon. Judith likely had banned her family from the room.

Cynthia felt herself being gently nudged forward. Aware of her father's hand in the small of her back, she moved into the room. Already Cal was saying, "This is Cynthia Longley," and the man occupying the plaid chair by the fireplace was rising to his feet. Cynthia let her eyes meet those of the attorney and wondered if he could read her mind. Did he know that she had been part of a plot to pair his widowed mother with her father? She felt her face warm as she reached to accept the offered hand.

Her father's turn to give the masculine hand a hearty shake meant that Cynthia, relieved, was able to turn away.

A slight rustle to her left brought her head around. A lively looking woman stepped through the door from the kitchen, a big apron wrapped around her small frame. Her face was flushed a rosy pink and her forehead looked slightly moist. But the honey-blond hair was perfectly coifed and a warm twinkle lit her blue eyes.

"And this is Mrs. Weston," Cal was

saying, indicating the bustling figure. Cynthia blinked. What was Mrs. Weston doing in Judith's kitchen — looking like she belonged? Looking very motherly.

The woman came forward, indicating the big apron with a good-natured sweep of her hand. "Judith was kind enough to find me one of her mother's aprons," she explained, still with that twinkle. "Dinner smells delicious. I never could stay out of kitchens."

She laughed, the sound soft and musical.

She wiped a hand on her apron before she extended it. "I do hope there's no gravy on it," she said with another chuckle. "You must be Cynthia, Judith's friend. I'm so happy to meet you."

Cynthia's head was spinning. Had she been able to paint a picture of the perfect woman for her father, it would have looked just like Mrs. Weston.

She accepted the hand and managed to mumble something she hoped made some kind of sense.

"And this is Paul Standard, Cynthia's father," Cal continued. She watched in awed silence as her father acknowledged the introduction and exchanged easy pleasantries with the widow lady.

"If you'll excuse me, Judith can use my help," the woman said with a warm smile that included them all, and she disappeared again through the kitchen door.

Cynthia managed to find her senses. "I'll . . . I'll give a hand too," she murmured to no one in particular and followed Mrs. Weston to Judith's kitchen.

She was afraid to look directly at Judith. Surely her own eyes would betray her secret. Her astonishment. Her desire. She had promised not to meddle, and she had every intention of keeping that promise. Yet — it would be so hard. Not to encourage. Not to nudge a bit. Not to pry enough to find out just what her father was thinking about this new member of their congregation.

Cynthia found a small task and busied herself. The two ladies working beside her chatted as though they were old friends. From the living room came the rumble of male voices, punctuated often by hearty laughter. Somewhere in the dim distance, children's voices called to one another. Cynthia knew they were in the basement family room, but she paid little attention to the rise and fall of childish chatter.

Before Cynthia had fully gathered her thoughts, Judith was asking Cal to call the children. The meal was ready to be served.

There was a good deal of commotion as the children, all five of them, scampered up from the basement and washed their hands at the bathroom sink as instructed. As the eldest and the only girl, Erin seemed to automatically take over. Soon she had her charges lined up, still-damp hands tucked behind their backs or fidgeting impatiently at their sides as they waited for grown-up instructions about where to sit.

Judith had managed to get eleven chairs around her dining room table. Cal announced the seating arrangements, and with a minimum of bustle and noise under the circumstances, they all found their places.

"This is so nice," spoke Mrs. Weston warmly after the grace was said, looking around with her bright smile. "I always wanted a big family. God didn't choose to bless us with one, but this . . . this is next best. Sharing with others."

"You have just the one son?" asked Cynthia's father, who sat next to her, thanks to Judith's arrangements.

"Just the one. But I couldn't ask for a better one." She gave her son a warm smile.

What else could a mother say? thought Cynthia. *I'd say the same* thing myself under similar circumstances.

"And I have just the one daughter," her father continued the conversation.

Cynthia prayed fervently that he wouldn't say she was the best he could possibly have. He didn't.

"And two grandsons," went on her father, proudly gracing Todd and Justin with a broad smile.

"Two grandsons," the woman repeated. "Well, you certainly are one up on me there. I can't wait for grandchildren. Must be so much fun."

"Oh, it is. Keeps me young. And busy." Cynthia's father was still smiling as he looked at his boys.

"It must be so much fun," the woman repeated.

Cynthia had the impression that Attorney Weston — P.C. — was stirring uneasily. She lifted her glance from her plate to give a brief peek in his direction. Yes, he did look a tad uncomfortable. He covered quickly by turning to Cal with a comment. Cynthia did not hear.

Judith had outdone herself with the meal. Everything was delicious and brought many comments from the diners. Even Todd exclaimed with young-boy frankness that "everything sure was good."

The conversation flowed easily. Cynthia found herself straining to get in on more than one discussion at a time. Her father and Mrs. Weston chatted easily throughout the meal, often addressing a remark to the entire table. She heard manly chuckles and feminine titters and marveled at how quickly they seemed to become acquainted with each other. Now and then Cynthia cast anxious little looks toward Judith, but her friend usually seemed occupied with her conversation with P. C. Weston and Cal. Cynthia did overhear Judith's favorite little joke about marrying Cal just so she could always be Wright. The attorney had grinned appreciatively.

Cynthia, seated between her two sons as she had requested, often missed bits of the conversation because of the chatter of her offspring and the Wright children. It was unnerving when she wanted to hear everything that was being said at the table.

After dessert the youngsters were excused and the grown-ups sat and enjoyed another cup of coffee. Conversation for the entire table was much easier then, and Cynthia enjoyed the chit-chat about current events and worldwide church news. She even voiced a few opinions, though mostly she was content to sit and listen.

She was the first to stir. Time was passing quickly. Her father always enjoyed a brief Sunday afternoon nap, a habit he had picked up since his retirement. At first he had done it, he said, to help the hours pass more quickly. Now he missed it if he didn't get his fifteen- or twenty-minute "power-nap," as he liked to call it. He would be getting restless if she didn't make a move to bring the delightful occasion to a close.

"Let me help with dishes," she

heard herself saying to Judith.

"Nonsense. Cal will help me."

Poor Cal, thought Cynthia. *It looks like he's already worked overtime.*

"Really," she insisted. "Let me give a hand."

Mrs. Weston was rising to her feet as well.

"It won't take long at all if we all pitch in," she said, gathering up dessert plates as she spoke. "Now, that was a mother's phrase if I ever heard one," she joked, and they joined in her laughter.

It seemed very natural for the three women to busy themselves in the kitchen together. In no time the cleanup task was done. Cynthia discovered that she secretly wanted it to last a bit longer. She was enjoying the cozy atmosphere of common-interest chatter and a shared task with other women. It reminded her of the good times she used to have with her mother. No wonder her father was so lonesome. *He lost the love and companionship of a truly wonderful woman,* Cynthia mused. She also missed it. That special camaraderie. She hadn't realized just how much until this moment. This moment of sharing, not just with Judith, but with this motherly woman who worked beside her.

Roger must have known, she found herself thinking. He had rather taken over after Mother died — coming to the kitchen to help, to chat, just to lean up against the counter and watch Cynthia fix a meal and casually discuss the happenings of the day. *He must have known,* she repeated inwardly. Now she did those tasks alone while her father entertained the boys.

But there was soon no reason to linger any longer in Judith's kitchen. Pensively she hung up the dish towel just as Mrs. Weston removed the ample apron from her Sunday dress.

"This has been fun," the older woman said, her voice indicating that the words were totally sincere. "I always longed for a daughter. Carl and I had planned a big family. We were so disappointed when that became impossible for us," the woman confided with a wistfulness in her voice. "But —" she added, picking up her cheerfulness again, "Preston has been a good son. He has given me so much joy."

He doesn't even want you around, Cynthia began a mental dialogue. *How could anybody not want you?* She could feel anger begin to smolder deep within her.

There seemed to be nothing to do now but to gather up her family and go home. Home to the house that had not really seemed like a home since Roger had died. They just lived there. Put in long days — and even longer nights. She did not look forward to the return.

Cynthia managed to be the last person to exit the door. She gave Judith an appreciative hug. They were not given to being "maudlin," as Judith called it, but Cynthia knew of no other way to let her longtime friend know how she felt.

"Thanks so much, Jude," she whispered.

To Cynthia's surprise, Judith held her for a moment. "So what do you think?" she asked in a return whisper.

Cynthia leaned back enough to see Judith's face as unbidden tears dimmed her eyes. "I don't know about Daddy," she murmured, "but I'd take her home today."

Judith grinned and gave Cynthia another squeeze. "Isn't she just adorable?"

Cynthia could only nod. Her heart

was too full for her to be able to speak.

"I was thinking," her father said on the drive home. "We really should return the invitation. Your mother was very particular about being hospitable — you know, in doing the turnabout. She never felt settled until she had returned the invitation."

Cynthia didn't respond and waited to see where he was going with this.

"Been a long time since we entertained," he continued.

Daddy, thought Cynthia, *we've never entertained.*

"Some folks are stepping out to a restaurant now instead of having people in their home. I still think that doing something at home is nice, but if you don't feel up to going to all that fuss, we can just offer to take them all out."

"The Wrights?"

He nodded.

They drove on in silence while Cynthia thought about his words. She knew he was right. They should "do the turnabout."

"Guess we could."

"Maybe when we get home we can sort of pick a Sunday," her father went on.

It was her turn to nod.

"Let's do it next Sunday," called Todd from the backseat.

"Yeah," seconded Justin. Both of them were full of enthusiasm about their friends and the toys in the Wright household.

"Next Sunday might be too soon," Cynthia cautioned. "It could sort of look like . . . like we wanted to hurry up and get it over with or something."

"A couple of Sundays then," said her father. He half turned to her. "Two Sundays between should be okay, shouldn't it?"

She nodded again. "I'll talk to Judith."

"I was thinking," said her father after a short pause. "Maybe we could invite the Westons too. They seem like real nice folks."

Cynthia turned her head to look at him. *You old rascal,* she thought to herself, a smile catching the corners of her mouth. *I'll just bet you do. I saw the way you two chatted throughout the entire meal.*

She looked out the side window of the car, no longer feeling threatened. Wouldn't it be wonderful if — ? But no — she would not allow her mind to jump ahead to such fancies. She would be too disappointed if it didn't happen.

"I'll call the Westons," she said, hoping that the excitement she was feeling would not be given away by her voice.

She saw her own soft smile transfer to her father's face.

It turned out to be three weeks before Cynthia hosted the Sunday dinner. When she had arrived home and studied her house, she had decided that she simply could not be ready any sooner. She had been neglectful. Though she was busy, in truth she had lost interest in housekeeping since Roger had died.

Now she looked about her with new

eyes. Things needed a good cleaning. The carpets were soiled. The draperies needed to be sent out. There were marks on the hall walls that needed paint touch-ups. The kitchen wallpaper looked shabby. The fireplace needed thorough attention.

Everywhere she looked she saw tasks that she had been neglecting.

She was grateful when her father informed her that he was willing to roll up his sleeves and go to work. For the first time since he'd retired, he looked excited about a project at hand.

On Monday she left a little list, and by the time she arrived home from work that evening, he had already completed many of the assignments. She fixed a hurried meal, changed into old jeans, and together they tackled the rest. The next day the routine was repeated. Cynthia soon found that with the brightening of her home, her spirits brightened as well. It felt great to see the rooms transformed. She was enjoying even straightening out drawers and closets — places that would not be on display for her guests, but knowing everything was orderly made her feel good. *I should have done this long ago,* she scolded herself and wondered just why she hadn't. How could she have let things get so far behind? But she'd not had enthusiasm for the tasks before. No compelling reason to take them on. It had been enough to just try to make it through each day.

"It looks great!" her father exclaimed with a broad smile when the very last item was scratched from the final list. Cynthia agreed. It did look good. She loved the new kitchen wallpaper. The borders that had been added to the boys' rooms. The freshness of the window treatments. The clean, unmarked paint on the walls. Even the carpet that she had longed to replace looked fresh and quite acceptable after the thorough shampooing.

"Sunday?"

"Sunday."

They stood there and grinned at each other.

The dinner went very well. Cynthia served a pot roast to rave reviews. The cherry pie was equally appreciated. The kids went off to play and the adults settled in the living room to chat, coffee cups in hand. After they moved from the subject of the weather to the main points of the morning's sermon, Cynthia noticed that the conversation on this occasion became more personal. More intimate.

"I don't feel too comfortable where I am now," Mrs. Weston admitted. "I'm thinking of selling that big house and moving. But it's hard, you know. That was our dream home, Carl's and mine. But he scarcely had time to enjoy it. It seems . . . strange . . . that things happen like that. It would have been so much better if I were still in the old house."

She hesitated a moment. "Then again — I likely never would have met any of you, and Carl would have never realized his dream. He always had in mind that I needed a more —

well, a larger, more impressive home. I was quite happy where I was. But he —" She stopped and smiled softly. "Guess men and women see things differently."

Cynthia's father nodded. "We do," he admitted. "I would've loved to have given Mary a nice, big house. One like she deserved. But it never happened. We lived in the same little home for all the twenty-nine years of our marriage."

"Twenty-nine years?"

Her father nodded.

"Carl and I were married for thirty-four."

Roger and I were only married for seven, Cynthia thought. *We were cheated.*

But Cynthia did not say the words. She even forced the thought from her mind. How could she think that way? God knew what was best in life — even in death.

"Well, one can cherish the memories of past days — but not live in them," the woman continued. "I thank God for each one of my special memories. But as good as they are, more than memories are needed to carry a person through the days. One must — eventually — learn to move on."

Her father nodded, but Cynthia thought that she still could read doubt in his eyes. It had been hard for her father to move on.

"So do you have any plans?" Cal, who had been listening thoughtfully, asked.

"No, not yet. But I like it here. I like the church, the pastor, the wonderful, busy seniors' program. The feel of . . . of warm family." She cast a glance toward her son. "I've been doing some thinking about moving here."

Cynthia also took a quick peek at P. C. Weston. She did not see him flinch. Saw no shadow of concern in his eyes. She could not read his face at all. Was he at all at odds with his mother's comment?

"I think that would be wonderful," her father was saying. By the look in his eyes, he was very enthusiastic about the idea.

"We'd love to have you," Judith put in. "It already feels like you belong. It's hard to remember that you've only been with us for a few weeks."

Mrs. Weston reached out and clasped Judith's hand in her right and

Cynthia's in her left. "I feel that way too," she said simply. "You two have made me feel so at home."

It was time to do the dishes.

Four weeks later the Westons issued an invitation. The little party was to get together again.

"Preston's apartment is far too small to host a dinner," Mrs. Weston explained. "So we are going to a restaurant. Then we will go back to his place for dessert and coffee."

No one complained about the arrangement.

The restaurant meal was a wonderful treat. The Westons had chosen the best place in town. With no need for the hostess to be jumping up to serve or to clear the plates, all of them settled in to enjoy the food and the conversation.

When the meal was over there was no lingering over coffee, no playroom to which to send the kids. The attorney settled the bill and Mrs. Weston pushed her chair back.

"We must get these youngsters away from the table and give them some running room," she said. "They have been sitting quite long enough."

Her smile included all five. "You have behaved so nicely. I'm proud of you."

The kids squirmed in embarrassed pleasure.

They had done well, Cynthia agreed as she pushed away from the table. Even her Todd and Justin. But she was a little nervous now. What would happen at the bachelor apartment? How would the immaculate attorney respond to five active, noisy kids romping through his quarters? She wished they could just go on home and leave the event on a positive note.

Just as she feared, when they were invited to step through the door, everything in the apartment spoke of expensive taste and extreme orderliness. Cynthia held her breath.

"You youngsters. Check the closet there," Mrs. Weston said as she bustled in. "Preston did some shopping so you'd have something to do while we visit."

The kids needed no second invitation. They bounded toward the closet and fell to their knees. Indeed the attorney had done some shopping. Cynthia's mouth opened in surprise. She had never seen such up-to-date toys. They were not many in number but carefully chosen. She quickly spotted two new motorized space station building sets that her boys had begged for as Christmas gifts — and she had been unable to supply. There was also a small train set, complete with tracks and a village to construct.

Erin, too, had been considered. Quietly she took schoolteacher Barbie with her potential classroom and went off to a corner to set up the scene.

The boys expressed enthusiasm and dived in with noisy excitement. Cynthia noticed the attorney smile softly. He seemed pleased with their pleasure.

Maybe it was self-protection rather than generosity, thought Cynthia. He knew if they didn't have something to do they might — *But that's unfair,* she checked herself. It was kind of him to think of the kids.

The dessert, pound cake with strawberries and whipping cream, was delicious. They sat around the living room and drank rich, hot coffee and chatted while the kids continued to play with the new toys. Cynthia decided that it hadn't turned out too badly after all.

When it came time to go, the boys were disappointed. Reluctantly they began to gather up remote-controlled cars and the many connecting pieces and place them back in the box in the closet.

"They'll still be here when you come again," said the attorney. Cynthia glanced up. Was he serious? Was he actually considering letting them come again? Their social obligation was now covered. Was there to be another round?

Cynthia looked toward Judith. Her friend only smiled.

"It's really working quite well, don't you think? I mean, your dad and Mrs. Weston seem to really enjoy each other."

Cynthia smiled. "You're not going to believe this, but do you know what Daddy said the other day? He asked me to go shopping with him. Shopping! He hasn't added anything to his wardrobe since Mama died, except for the shirts, socks, and underwear that I pick up for him."

"Shopping? A man?"

"I couldn't believe it. I asked him just what he wanted, and he said —

with a rather embarrassed look — that he needed about everything. That he had let himself get pretty seedy. Imagine!"

"Well . . ." said Judith, raising an eyebrow. "Maybe things are moving along faster than we would have dared to think."

"I hope they don't move too fast," Cynthia said soberly. "I mean, I think she's great, but I want them both to be sure."

"They're not kids — either one of them," Judith reminded.

"I know, but . . . well . . . you never can be too cautious. I've known of two perfectly wonderful people who just didn't work out together at all."

Judith nodded her agreement, then said, "So, any future plans? Dinners? Outings?"

"Daddy and P.C. are taking the boys to the hockey game next Friday night."

"He likes hockey?"

"You're surprised?"

Judith shrugged. "I guess I am . . . a bit. I mean, he seems more like the kind who would be into — I dunno — polo. Cricket."

They looked at each other and fought to control their giggles.

Cynthia became serious again. "Guess he likes most every sport — according to Daddy."

"So the two men will be going off with the boys to this hockey thing. Then what? More events? More outings?"

"I suppose."

"And you don't mind?"

Cynthia looked up, not sure what the question implied. "What do you mean — mind? It's good for boys to have — to be with men. Daddy has always said so. I'm glad that someone is willing to take them. Sports are good for them — except wrestling. I draw the line at wrestling. I never could understand grown men —"

"And what do you do?"

Cynthia set her coffee cup down. "What do you mean?"

"If these . . . these males in your life spend their time running to . . . to sports things, what do *you* do?"

Cynthia frowned. She had not thought about the lonely nights sitting at home by herself. It was not an enjoyable prospect.

"Maybe you should find something to do with Mrs. Weston," Judith went on.

"Could you join us?"

Even though Cynthia was learning to care deeply for the older woman, she was not quite prepared to take full responsibility for the friendship.

"I have a family," answered Judith simply. "Friday night is our family night. The kids always look forward to planning the activity. They plan way ahead. Next Friday we are going bowling."

"Oh, fun."

"You could join us. Cal wouldn't mind."

For a moment Cynthia was tempted but she quickly shook her head. "I couldn't," she said lamely. "It would feel very . . . odd. My father taking the boys out and me going off on my own."

"Another time then. Maybe you all can join us."

Cynthia turned back to her pastry. It did sound like fun, but after all, family outings were special and meant to be just that. It would change things if she horned in.

She looked up at Judith and smiled her thanks but made no commitment.

When spring came, Mrs. Weston decided to go home and put her big house up for sale. Cynthia knew that she would miss her. It wouldn't be the same without her cheerful smile greeting them each Sunday.

"This is late notice," the diminutive woman said on her last Sunday with them, "but could you go out for dinner? I'm going to miss you all so much, and I thought that we should spend one more —"

"Yes!" Todd drew back a fist and pumped it enthusiastically.

"I do have a roast in —" Cynthia started to explain.

"I can run home and remove it from the oven," her father said quickly.

Cynthia smiled. "Well," she said, "it sounds like the family is much more interested in your invitation than in eating at home — so, yes, thank you."

"I have my car. Preston came early for the men's prayer time before the service. I'll meet you at Dixon's," Mrs. Weston instructed. "I'll go on ahead and have them set up the table."

"Dixon's." Cynthia nodded, watching as Mrs. Weston hurried away to her car.

"C'mon, Grandpa Paul," prompted Justin. "Let's go take out the roast."

Her father moved to follow the two eager boys, then turned back to Cynthia. "No need for you to come. We'll just turn off the roast and meet you at Dixon's."

"But . . . how am I to —"

"You can ride with P.C." And he was gone.

Cynthia felt her cheeks coloring. How was she going to go to the attorney and say that she had been left behind? But he suddenly was there beside her. "Ready?" was all he said. She nodded, relieved that she hadn't needed to ask.

I could go with Judith and Cal, she found herself thinking as they left the church and proceeded across the parking lot. But she knew they always had a full van, what with their own brood and picking up neighborhood children for the Sunday service.

P.C. opened the car door and she settled herself on the smooth dark leather of the seat. The car even smelled clean. Cynthia thought of her own vehicle. It had been years since it had looked polished. Not since Roger . . . She really needed to give it a good cleaning. In fact, she really was in need of a newer car. If it wasn't for her father . . .

"Good sermon," he began as he backed from the parking spot.

Cynthia nodded.

"Mother really enjoys the services here."

"That's nice," mumbled Cynthia.

He smiled. He really had a pleasant smile when he chose to use it.

"But then, that's not all she enjoys." Her eyes widened as she tried to figure out if there was some kind of hidden message in the words.

"I've been hoping for an opportunity to talk with you — alone — for some time," he went on and Cynthia blinked.

He grinned. "There sure isn't any opportunity when we are in our little crowd."

No, there was not. She wondered if they had said more than a dozen words to each other over the past months. But the fact had not concerned her. Not in the least.

"I've been wondering . . . if you . . . well, if you feel like I do?"

Cynthia squirmed on the leather seat and held her breath. What in the world did the man mean?

"What do you think? Maybe I shouldn't even say it — or *think* it — but does it seem to you that Mother and your father might be just a little . . . attracted to each other?"

Cynthia let the air release in a little gasp and turned to look fully at him. She could feel the flush of her cheeks. But since he was asking an honest question — with seriousness — she felt obligated to answer. She swallowed hard and nodded slightly.

"I . . . I certainly believe that Daddy thinks your mother is a . . . a delightful woman," she managed to say.

"Would it upset you if anything were to come of it?"

"Oh no," said Cynthia quickly. "I quite like your mother."

He smiled.

"Would it . . . would it . . . upset

you?" she asked in turn.

"Me?" His smile broadened. "On the contrary. It would ease my mind considerably."

Why? she wondered inwardly as she faced forward again. Didn't this man realize how blessed he was to have such a wonderful mother?

"It's been great for me — having Mother here," he explained, as if Cynthia had spoken her thoughts. "But I don't think living with me is the life she needs. She needs . . . more. She is a beautiful, intelligent, talented woman. She needs to learn to be able to give of herself again. Frankly, living with me is not enough to fill her days. She needs . . . people . . . activities . . . a place of service. She isn't likely to find that if she stays on with me."

Cynthia turned questioning eyes on him. "You don't think so?"

"I'm sure of it. She spends all her time fussing. Over little things. Things that don't really matter. She needs more than small, cramped quarters and one bachelor son. A challenge. A bigger world."

"But . . . she's going to sell her house."

"I know. That concerns me. Oh . . . not that she's going to sell her house. That's the right move, I think. But then what? Cooped up in my apartment all day? I don't think that would be good for her."

"I . . . I'm afraid I don't follow —" Cynthia began.

"I thought we might — sort of — join forces."

Cynthia frowned. Where was this

conversation going?

"They do seem to enjoy each other. I have a great deal of respect for your father. He's the kind of man — well, frankly, I wouldn't mind Mother becoming . . . involved."

"But —"

"Of course, they must make up their own mind. I don't want to force anything. But still, if they had just a —" He grinned again and held up a thumb and finger, indicating a small space. "If they had just a little bit of encouragement — I mean if they knew that we were in favor, then they might not be reluctant to explore —" he hesitated a moment, then finished with, "the possibility."

"I don't know," Cynthia began slowly. "It sounds —"

"Nothing manipulative," he cut

into her thoughts, then quickly added, "Of course, if you are doubtful, if you don't think Mother —"

"Oh no. It's not that. It's just — well — I don't want to interfere."

"Nor do I. But I wouldn't mind giving, what should I say, assent."

"And how could we do that?"

"Mother will be back here — soon, I hope. I am hopeful that it won't take long to sell her house. She thinks the world of you — and the boys. It wouldn't be at all hard to — well, to arrange for little outings, and then give them some space to talk . . . to get to know each other better."

Cynthia thought about it and nodded. "That I can agree to," she said simply.

"Maybe some days I could take the boys off to . . . something . . . and let the two have the day to themselves."

Cynthia thought about that awhile. What could an attorney manage to think up for her two boys? "Like . . . what?" she finally asked.

"I don't know . . . yet. Todd has been talking of a go-cart. Might be fun to help him build one."

"He'd love it," Cynthia responded before she could stop herself.

"I have a friend with a garage. He'd let us use it. Maybe Justin would like to work on it too."

"I'm sure he would."

They were pulling into the restaurant parking lot. He turned to her. "Then it's a deal? Our little secret?" He was smiling again.

"A deal," she responded, reflecting the smile. "Encouragement. No manipulation. I promised God I wouldn't try to take things into my own hands."

"You did?" He looked into her face with obvious interest. Cynthia felt herself flush again.

"I . . . I admit I wanted Daddy to find . . . someone. But I realized that I was wrong to . . . to try to work it out. Then your mother came. I really do like her. A lot. But I won't —"

"I'll honor your promise," he said with sincerity. "I won't ask anything that you are uncomfortable with. Honest. We'll just give them occasioned opportunities and see what happens."

Cynthia nodded. It seemed they had an understanding, a common goal.

Chapter Four

Some Minor Adjustments

Mrs. Weston did not wait around for her home to sell but left it in the hands of a capable realtor and returned to her son's apartment. "I couldn't stand the loneliness," she informed Cynthia confidentially. Cynthia nodded. She would not wish to be all alone in a big house either.

You shouldn't be alone, Cynthia wanted to say. *You really do need to find someone.* And Cynthia was quite sure in her heart that she knew just the one.

Now that P.C. was also thinking in the same direction, it shouldn't be too difficult to at least give the idea a chance.

P.C. was already spending many evenings working with the boys on the go-cart. They had set up shop in his friend's garage, and after the day's work and school, they spent most of their free time there. Her father hung around with them, seeming to enjoy the whole experience as much as his grandsons.

Cynthia popped in on the little group one evening to inform her father that she would be at Judith's for an hour or so to go over some Sunday school materials. She was mildly shocked to see the immaculate attorney, old blue jeans and ratty T-shirt streaked with grease, hair flopping forward over one eye, a smear across his forehead, and a rather ridiculous grin on his face. "Always wanted to do this," he admitted, "but never had any valid reason."

Cynthia shook her head. In their excitement at seeing the go-cart take shape, all four of them were acting like a bunch of schoolboys.

When the go-cart was completed, they turned their attention to other things. P.C. joined the fishing trips, the ball games, the sand-lot Saturday practice. He even took her father's place, signing up as the adult accompanying the boys on the Brigade

camping trip. "My bones are getting too old to sleep on the ground," her father had cheerfully conceded.

"How can we ever get the two adults together when Daddy is busy running off with P.C. and the boys all the time?" Cynthia complained to Judith while they sipped Saturday coffee. "This all was supposed to . . . to make opportunity for Daddy and his mother. But Mrs. Weston and I are off shopping or baking cookies while the men —"

"Tell him," responded Judith. "Tell P.C. that was the whole purpose of the . . . the getting together with your boys."

"I . . . I hate to talk to him about it. I mean, I really don't know him that well."

"You've got to tell him. Lay it on the line. He's supposed to be helping the process — not hindering it."

Cynthia nodded. She would try to find some way of bringing up the subject with P.C.

"May I talk with you," she finally managed as the two of them moved down the church steps the next Sunday.

He stopped and smiled encouragingly. She knew he expected her to say what was on her mind right then and there. She shook her head, nervousness knotting her stomach.

"Not . . . here. Not now. Sometime when . . ."

His smile disappeared as he nodded. "When?"

"Can we . . . can we meet for coffee or something — ?"

"Have I done something?" he asked quickly, his words little more than a whisper. There were many others from the congregation within earshot.

"No. I mean, not really. Look, I don't want a conversation right here. I mean —" She felt flushed and awkward.

"Coffee," he promised. "When?"

"Tonight? After the service? Daddy

will take the boys home."

He nodded. "Fine."

All the way home she worried and all afternoon she stewed. By the time they left for the evening service, she was sure that she had let Judith talk her into something foolish. She wished she could back out. What would he think of her? It was just plain silly. But she had already made the . . . the date. Her father was all set to take the boys home and put them to bed.

She hardly heard a word of the sermon. What she did hear seemed not to register. By the time they were dismissed, her palms were sweaty and her throat was dry.

"I won't be late," she promised her father. Surely it couldn't take long to make some progress on the situation.

"Take your time," he said and smiled at her in a way she couldn't define.

"Ready?"

Cynthia looked up to discover P.C. standing next to her. *Ready?* Was she ready? No, she decided, *I certainly am not ready for this,* but she nodded her head dumbly and walked out with him to his leather-smelling car.

He talked easily as they drove.

Most of the conversation was about her boys, her father, the fun they were having together. She winced. This was exactly what she wanted to address. But she wouldn't do it now. Not yet. Not until they were settled in some dimly lit little cafe where he could not clearly see her face. Coffee cup in hand, she could summon up the courage to tell him that these boy-things had rather led him — led her father — off track.

He turned in to the parking lot of the Regency Hotel, and she saw at once that its cafe was brightly lit. She knew her face was not shadowed as she settled herself in the floral-printed booth. He asked for menus. But Cynthia had no desire for food. It would be hard enough to get the coffee down. He ordered coffee and pecan pie. She wondered fleetingly how he stayed so trim.

"Your boys —" he began.

"That's what I want to talk to you about," she hurried to say before she lost her nerve. His eyes widened. She knew he must have noticed the agitation in her voice.

"The boys? I've not done something, have I?"

"No. No . . . nothing like that. It's just —"

"I think your kids are great. I had hoped —"

"They think you're great too," Cynthia was quick to say.

He nodded at that, looking relieved. "I'm glad." Then he continued, his eyes deepening with intensity, "But you aren't comfortable with them being with me, is that it? But your father is always there, too, and —"

"That's not it," Cynthia tried to explain. She did wish she could get over her silly habit of blushing so easily. Her red cheeks always gave away her nervousness, her concern, or embarrassment. "Don't worry," she confessed. "I've had my eyes and ears open. I always talk to the boys. They know about telling if anything — anything — makes them . . . uneasy. They have told me all about your outings. I feel no concern about them being with you. And of course Daddy has been there, or some of the church group."

He nodded. She could see that he understood perfectly her duty as a responsible parent. She had checked on him, yet she knew he didn't blame her.

"So . . . it's something else?"

She nodded. She reached for the coffee spoon and toyed with it the way that always annoyed Judith. She caught herself and laid it aside.

"That's just it. You . . . and the boys — and Daddy — you're always off doing things together — just the four of you."

He was listening to her closely. "We've been leaving you out, haven't we?" There was apology in his voice.

She stared at him a moment. "That's not it. Not — I mean, I thought this whole . . . whole idea was to give Daddy and your mother — well — a chance to get to know each other. But it's been a . . . a totally male thing. The fact that you boys go off and your mother and I do something, that's no way to . . . to —"

She couldn't finish. She was flushing again.

He appeared to be thinking seriously about what she was saying. At length he nodded. "You're absolutely right," he said. "I've been . . . selfish. I've been enjoying the boys and your father and I'd almost forgotten what — I'm truly sorry."

And he did sound sorry. And look sorry.

Cynthia shifted uneasily on the seat just as the waiter returned to refill the cups. She waited until he moved away.

"I'm glad you've enjoyed the boys," she said. "They . . . they have really been having a great time. It's been good for them. But —"

"Can we start over?" he asked candidly, almost pleading in his tone.

Cynthia looked up and forced a crooked smile. Maybe she should have let things take their own course. After all, the men and boys seemed to be having a wonderful time together.

"I'm sorry too," she said sincerely, shaking her head ruefully. "I do appreciate your interest in the boys. I shouldn't have even —"

"No. You're right. We need to . . . to spend more time together. All of us. Do more family-type things. There are lots of things that —"

He stopped and looked at her steadily. A grin spread across his face. "You like fishin'?" he asked, and her answer was a look of mock horror.

It maybe was a little awkward at first, but soon they all settled into an easy rhythm of family outings.

Cynthia even dared to think that it would not take many months for their goal to be realized. Her father and Mrs. Weston seemed to thoroughly enjoy each other's company. And with every outing, the bond among all of them was strengthened.

But perhaps . . . perhaps it was the two boys who were, unconsciously, the ones to bring the two widowed people together. It was very natural for the four of them to be drawn into a little group on their outings, one boy attached to each adult — discovering things, attempting things, enjoying things.

Cynthia and P.C. exchanged expectant smiles.

"We need to let them get off alone now and then," he whispered to her on one such occasion.

"But how? Daddy always expects the boys to tag along with him whenever he's around."

He frowned. "Then we'll need to plan things with the boys — and leave Mother and your dad free to do something else."

"What?"

"I don't know. We'll find something. Have you been to the city zoo lately?"

"No."

"There. There's one outing right there." He grinned with satisfaction.

"What if they want to come?"

This brought back the perplexed look. "Leave it to me," he said with confidence but still looking thoughtful.

Cynthia nodded. She would leave it to him.

★ ★ ★

Gradually, along with the group activities, there came times when Cynthia and P.C. took the boys off on one or another outing — slyly suggesting what their parents might wish to do with the free time. And then on occasion Cynthia and P.C. requested a bit of free time of their own, coming up with a plausible reason and asking if their parents would baby-sit the boys. The two youngsters still seemed to be the best allies in drawing the two together.

Both Cynthia and P.C. were even more sure of that following a conversation they overheard between Justin and Mrs. Weston one afternoon.

"Would you be my grandma?" the boy had asked wistfully. "I don't got a grandma."

The woman had pulled Justin close to her side and held him. "I would love to," she responded, tears in her eyes. Cynthia caught the look that quickly passed between the woman and her father.

"You can't," put in the officious Todd. "Grandmas are family."

"Maybe we can find a way." Mrs. Weston managed to address Todd's comment and ease Justin's concern with the few words.

"Right now?" asked the usually patient Justin, a shine lighting his eyes.

"If you're in a hurry, perhaps we can just . . . sort of pretend."

"I don't want to just pretend. I want it to be real."

Justin's lip quivered and Mrs. Weston quickly said, "Then I guess we'd better make it official — now.

There's more than one way to become family."

Todd looked doubtful.

"Have you ever heard of adoption?" she inquired of the two boys.

Justin nodded. He had a friend who had been adopted, whatever that meant.

"That's a decision that folks make to take someone into the family. Make them a real part of it," explained the woman.

"Does it work?" asked Todd.

"Sure it works. You run and find a nice sheet of paper and a pencil."

Justin hurried off to do as bidden.

"This will do until my son makes it official," Mrs. Weston explained to Todd as they waited.

Todd cast a questioning look toward the man.

"That's the kind of work attorneys do," Mrs. Weston went on. "That and other things."

Todd nodded, his expression indicating that if a real lawyer worked on it, he was sure it would be all right.

Justin, soon back, handed the pencil and paper to Mrs. Weston. Soon she had completed the written document to her satisfaction.

"Now, I sign here — and you sign there," she informed the boy. "This is just temporary, you understand. Someday we'll have to make it legal — one way or another."

Cynthia and P.C. exchanged glances again.

Justin didn't bother to ask further questions. With a grin he reached for the pencil and printed his name on the line indicated.

"Can you — can I put my name on it too?" asked Todd rather hesitantly.

It was done. Mrs. Weston announced with a smile, "Now you can call me Grandma Dee." Both boys ran off, noisy in their excitement.

Accepting the woman at her word, from then on they referred to her as Grandma Dee. Cynthia thought the woman actually glowed each time they spoke her new title.

"I didn't know your mother's name was Dusteen," Cynthia commented as she and P.C. drove into the city for dinner.

"I'm surprised you found out," he answered. "She never has liked it. Says it's a silly name. She always goes by Dee."

"She signed it as 'Dusteen' on the

adoption paper."

He smiled. "Wow! She really was being official."

"Are you . . . are you actually going to draw up legal papers?" she asked as she turned to him.

"What do you think?" His smile broadened. "Shall we just sort of take our time and see what happens? As Mother said, there's more than one way to make it official." He winked. "Things seem to be moving rather nicely, don't you think?"

She nodded, her satisfaction reflected on her face. It did seem that way.

"Rather strange," Cynthia said, her thoughts taking another turn. "Your mother's name is Dusteen and she uses Dee. Your name is Preston and —"

"I've never liked Preston. Apologies to my parents, their extraordinary common sense did not seem to be at work when it came to naming me." They exchanged a knowing grin.

"Have you ever thought of using your second name? Many people do," Cynthia suggested.

"My father was Carl. Two Carl Westons in the same law firm could be rather confusing."

She nodded. "I guess it would be."

They rode in silence, the radio playing softly, blending in with the smooth hum of the motor.

"But you could use it now," Cynthia finally ventured.

He looked at her awhile, then agreed with a nod of his head. "Could, couldn't I?"

She watched his face. He seemed to like the idea.

"Think I will. I like that. Never was crazy about 'P.C.' but didn't know what else to do. Carl Weston. I like that. I think Dad would too."

He reached across the seat and gave her hand a squeeze. "Thanks," he said with a smile.

Cynthia flushed slightly. She had only suggested what seemed to be perfectly natural.

"So how's it going?"

The two women sat with steaming coffee cups before them, picking daintily at their carrot cake — a concession on Cynthia's part because of their careful watching of calories over the weeks — and Judith spoke the words, one eyebrow lifted as she posed the question.

Cynthia tried not to sound smug. "Good. I think they really do enjoy each other."

"I've noticed."

Cynthia looked up at the terse comment but let it pass.

"And the boys really love her. Even call her Grandma Dee."

"I know. I've heard them."

They each were silent for a few minutes.

"How do you feel about it?" Judith finally asked.

"Me?"

Judith nodded.

Cynthia was thoughtful. Almost yearning. "I hadn't realized how much I've missed Mama. It's so special to be able to share time with a motherly — mothering — woman.

She just understands . . ."

"So you aren't sorry? That we got involved? Sort of."

Cynthia looked at her friend's teasing expression, then smiled and shook her head. She could not deny her own feelings. She already loved Mrs. Weston like a mother. Nothing would make her happier than her father deciding to — but she must not rush things. She turned her attention back to Judith.

"If it happens I will be thrilled," she said simply.

"What do you mean, 'if'? When."

"I'm still not interfering, Jude, even though I might wish to."

Judith nodded.

"And you're no longer concerned with your father being involved with the mother of Sober Preston Weston?"

Cynthia's cheeks flushed. She stirred uneasily. "You were right," she finally admitted, facing Judith. "I judged too quickly. He's really not like that, at all. He's —" The color in her cheeks deepened. "Cal was right. He is fun. He does have an appealing sense of humor. And he's — you know, I was upset with him for not wanting his mother in his life. But he's really very sweet with her. Honest. In fact" — her color intensified again — "he's really very thoughtful . . . with everyone."

Judith said nothing, but Cynthia noticed a knowing look in her eyes.

"Okay," she admitted with a shrug of her shoulders. "You were right. I've said it. Are you going to make me crawl? I've learned my lesson. One should never, ever, prejudge another."

Judith smiled.

"And, by the way, he's going by 'Carl' now. I . . . I sort of suggested it."

Judith smiled again.

Fall came and their excursions shifted to accommodate the change of weather. When winter arrived, they shifted once again. From picnics and ball games they went to bowling and sleigh rides. Sunday dinners were usually spent together, from time to time including Judith, Cal, and the kids. Judith began to make little re-marks. "As I've said before, I'm always Wright," she stated pointedly more than once.

Cynthia just smiled. It was good to feel like one large family. She had needed that sense of belonging. Of being family again. Cynthia made sure she kept the Saturday morning date for coffee. She still needed Judith's friendship even though she no longer felt so lonely.

No one even lifted an eyebrow when Carl, as he was now known, and his mother changed location in the church sanctuary. They now joined Paul Standard, his daughter, Cynthia, and her two boys over on the right side.

And no one seemed a bit surprised, though many expressed great delight, when the announcement came that there was to be a Christmas wedding. Judith hugged Cynthia warmly, the tears on her cheeks mingling with Cynthia's own.

But of all the people who rejoiced, no one did so more enthusiastically than young Justin.

"Now you'll *really* be my grandma," he exclaimed as he threw his arms around the older woman's neck. "We won't even need to have new papers made, will we?"

She hugged him close, the tears brightening her eyes. "No papers necessary. God has His own way of working things out."

Justin nodded, his head close up against her. "It's the very, very best way," he said with great assurance.

"I quite agree. The very best way," she said as she squeezed him tighter.

Todd crowded close to be included in the embrace. "And you're my grandma too," he reminded her.

"Your grandma too." Her arm reached out to encircle him and draw him close.

"I like it," he said. "I like being real family."

Cynthia blinked back joyful tears. Todd had spoken her heart as well.

Chapter Five

A Match Made in Heaven

"It turned out rather well, don't you think?" he said.

"Wonderfully!"

He chuckled softly. "Had me worried for a while. Sort of dragged their feet."

She was still smiling when she replied, "Well, they had to be sure. I think, all in all, it rather caught them both off guard."

"Didn't take them long once they'd made up their minds."

"Three weeks."

He chuckled again. " 'Course they knew each other pretty well by then, and the boys were pushing for it."

"They're so excited, aren't they?" She reached to pour him another cup of coffee.

"Funny how these things work sometimes," he noted as he added a touch of sugar.

"Would be funny, if one didn't realize that God has His plans."

He nodded.

"It was a lovely wedding, didn't you think?" she continued.

"Awfully small."

"Yes — small, but so . . . so intimate and sweet."

"She had a big, big church wedding the first time. I don't think she wanted any reminders of that," he commented.

They were seated in Cynthia's kitchen, the winter sun brushing past the frilly curtains to illuminate the soft yet rich colors of the almost-new wallpaper.

"I like to think that God had just a bit of help from us," he grinned teasingly.

From the room beyond came the chatter of the two boys as they busied themselves with their new Christmas toys. It all seemed so homey.

She sipped at her morning coffee. "When did you know? I mean, when did you think that they might finally

be interested in one another?" She smiled softly.

He gave it some thought. "I guess that time she slipped on the icy sidewalk and he reached out and — you know — sort of held on to her." He demonstrated. "I thought to myself that he could have let go much sooner than he did." His eyes twinkled.

"I first noticed it that time we all went to play tennis in the fall, and he was showing her how to hold the racquet."

He nodded. "I thought that seemed a little fakey," he said with a snort, then a smile. "True, she hasn't played tennis for a while, but she used to play. I didn't think she could have forgotten that much."

"Well, he didn't seem to mind giving her a lesson."

"And she wasn't catching on too soon either."

They both laughed.

"You should have seen him when he told me they were planning to be married," she said. "I've never seen him so . . . so alive. He said, 'I've found the one with whom I want to share the rest of my life.' I didn't have to ask any questions."

"And she walked around here in a

daze. Thought her feet would never come back to ground. The boys were silly-excited. Yelling and hollering and calling up friends. I don't know when I've seen two kids more thrilled about anything."

She looked thoughtfully out the window, then added, with a warm big smile on her face, "It's been fun watching it happen, hasn't it?"

"You think everything is fun." His eyes twinkled appreciatively.

With misty eyes she said, "I'm beginning to — again."

"Grandma Dee," said Justin, entering the room munching on a sticky bun. He paused a moment, then said, "When will Mama and Dad be back from their — the moon thing?"

"Honeymoon." Todd yelled the correction from the room beyond.

"Honeymoon," repeated Justin.

"Sunday. Your . . . your father has to be back at work on Monday."

"But Mama's not going back to work?"

"No. Your mama will be staying home now."

A big grin lit his face. "Good," he said.

He leaned up against her, and she reached up and brushed back his hair.

"But you'll still be here?" he asked with some concern in his voice.

"Oh my, yes. You'll never get rid of me now."

The boy's grin broadened.

"Not right in this house," she went on to explain. "Not like I am now. I'm just here until your folks get home. Your grandpa dropped by for breakfast to make sure you were okay. But I'll be close by. You can be sure of that."

The youngster seemed satisfied. He gave her a quick hug and left to resume his play, calling over his shoulder as he went, "Boy, I can hardly wait to have my own real daddy at home."

The two returned to their coffee in silence, a musing smile playing on both sets of lips. Paul shifted and spoke. "What are your plans, Dee? Will you stay on in P.C.'s — Preston's — Carl's — whatever his name is — ?" He waved a hand and rolled his eyes, and she laughed.

"It is rather confusing," she admitted. "But I guess we'll get used to it."

"Anyway, will you keep his apartment?"

"No. I won't live there. It's much too . . . too masculine and austere. Nothing homey about it, as far as I'm concerned. It was all I could do to manage over the last months. If it hadn't been for our little secret mission, I think I would have moved out to a place of my own."

"Well — 'mission accomplished,' as they say. Guess you can make your own plans now."

"I have. And I feel at rest that I've done the right thing."

There was a pause while he waited for her to go on.

"I've already signed up for a new senior condo in Meadowdale."

"You have?"

"Oh . . . they are nice. Have you looked at them?"

"No."

"You should. You might like them. And there are all sorts of special facilities there. Swimming pool. Lawn bowling. Exercise room. It's nice. You might decide to sell your house and —"

"I'm not quite ready to sell — not yet. Got a lot of fixing up to do. It's been rather neglected the last while. It seemed to take all my time to keep things up for Cynthia." He sighed. "And I admit — I didn't feel much like hanging around an empty house or fixing things."

She nodded understandingly.

"My new apartment's not ready until March," she continued.

"So what will you do until then?"

"I've given it a lot of thought and I think that — well, it would be better if — they should have some space.

There will be adjustments. Bound to be. Cynthia doesn't need a mother-in-law looking over her shoulder in the next few weeks."

He nodded. "I should make myself scarce too," he agreed.

"I've decided to take a trip," she explained. "Three of the ladies from the church are going on a little tour of Europe. I've decided to go along and make it a foursome."

"That will be nice."

"I've always wanted to travel. I figure now is a good time to get started. Carl and I had planned . . ." But she let the sentence go unfinished. "What about you?" she asked instead.

His mouth began to work slowly and a twinkle glinted in his eyes. They had become such good friends over the last months of engineering

things to get their offspring finally together and settled that they could
share just about anything. And now
they were family.

"I haven't told a soul," he admitted, "but I have — sort of — been seeing Evie Winguard."

Her eyes widened. "When on earth
did you find time for that?"

He shook his head. "Hasn't been
easy."

She laughed then, a soft, delighted
sound.

"Haven't been able to pay near as
much attention as she deserves, but
now that the kids are settled I feel —
well, I plan to . . ." He actually turned
red.

She reached out and took the hand
that rested on the table. "I think
that's just wonderful, Paul," she ex-

claimed. "I really like Evie. She's a sweet, thoughtful lady." Then she added with just a hint of tears in her eyes, "And a very lucky one too. I wish you both the best."

He squeezed her hand. He knew she was sincere.

"Maybe someday you'll find —"

"Oh, don't even say it. I'm not ready for that yet. Maybe I never will be. But anyway, I'm quite — what does one say? — quite content. Now that Carl is married, now that I finally have my daughter — and grandsons — life looks pretty good. I'm actually excited about it. I'm finally ready to settle in and enjoy it — again."

They exchanged a smile, now both blinking back the tears of joy. He nodded, a silent prayer of gratitude swelling within his heart. "Like you said — with just a little help from us, it all turned out rather well."

Janette Oke was born in Champion, Alberta, during the Depression years, to a Canadian prairie farmer and his wife. She is a graduate of Mountain View Bible College in Didsbury, Alberta, where she met her husband, Edward. They were married in May of 1957, and went on to pastor churches in Indiana as well as Calgary and Edmonton, Canada.

The Okes have three sons and one daughter and are enjoying the addition of grandchildren to the family. Edward and Janette have both been active in their local church, serving in various capacities as Sunday school teachers and board members. They make their home near Calgary, Alberta.

We hope you have enjoyed this Large Print book. Other Thorndike Press or Chivers Press Large Print books are available at your library or directly from the publishers.

For more information about current and up-coming titles, please call or write, without obligation, to:

Thorndike Press
P.O. Box 159
Thorndike, Maine 04986 USA
Tel. (800) 223-1244
Tel. (800) 223-6121

OR

Chivers Press Limited
Windsor Bridge Road
Bath BA2 3AX
England
Tel. (0225) 335336

All our Large Print titles are designed for easy reading, and all our books are made to last.